Books by the same author
The Sniff Stories
Sniff Bounces Back
Sniff and the Secret of Spalderton Hall

Picture Books
Quacky Quack-quack!

IAN WHYBROW

MOLLY and the SKYBOARD

Illustrations by Tony Kenyon

WALKER BOOKS
LONDON

*For my darling niece, Holly Jones Warren,
who dreamed it all up*
I. W.

First published 1993 by
Walker Books Ltd, 87 Vauxhall Walk
London SE11 5HJ

Text © 1993 Ian Whybrow
Illustrations © 1993 Tony Kenyon

This book has been typeset in ITC Garamond.

Printed in England by Clays Ltd, St Ives plc

British Library Cataloguing in Publication Data
A catalogue record for this book is
available from the British Library.

ISBN 0-7445-2428-8

Contents

Chapter One

On the morning of Holly's seventh birthday, Holly got up and did her chores as usual, even though it was her special day.

When she felt she'd done a good job, she opened her present from her mum and dad. It was a hand-knitted pullover with a skateboard pattern on the front.

Holly said it would look good with her red hair.

"Sorry we couldn't afford a real skateboard," sighed Dad. He knew how much Holly had wanted one.

Her mum said, "There's a lovely surprise for you today. Guess what! Your cousin Richard is coming over to play with you! Won't that be nice?"

Holly didn't like telling lies, but her mum looked so pleased, she couldn't hurt her feelings. "Just what I wanted on my birthday!" she said bravely.

Richard arrived in a big car driven
by his nanny. He was a big rude boy
with a big bottom. He was carrying
the most *unbelievably* expensive
skateboard in the whole world, all
covered in fabulous stickers.

He also had a very small package
which he gave to Holly.

"Here you are, Carrot Head," he said. "It's a book of stamps. Don't forget to stick one on your thank you letter, will you? Good joke, eh?" And he laughed, blah ha ha!

I wish he wouldn't call me Carrot Head, thought Holly.

Chapter Two

Five minutes after Richard arrived, he said, "This is so *boring*! What are we supposed to do all day when you haven't even got a telly in this dump?"

"Why don't we go skateboarding?"
Holly suggested. Every night, ever
since she could remember, Holly
had dreamed about skateboards.

In the dream she had a skateboard
with magic buttons on it. If she
wanted to do a fantastic trick, all
she had to do was press a button.

She looked longingly at Richard's skateboard, hoping that perhaps he would let her try it out.

"No way!" Richard snapped. "I bet you haven't even got a skatepark here or anything."

Holly said no, they didn't have a skatepark, but there was a quiet bit of roadway out the back. "Why don't we go and see?" she said.

There was a good slope that went
down and down, then up in front of
some big blue garage doors.

"There are some super bumpy
parts here," said Holly. "They would
be fun for lying down. And there's
a drain to dodge by the kerb."

"What do you know about it, *girly*?" said Richard. "And what does that stupid old man want?"

Holly turned to see her next door neighbour, Mr Windrush, waving to her over his back gate. "Happy Birthday, Holly," he called. "Would you and your cousin like to come into the workshop and see the present I've made for you?"

"*I'm* not coming!" shouted Richard. "I hate home-made presents!" And with that, he jumped on his fancy skateboard and whizzed off down the slope.

Chapter Three

Holly ran over to the gate. "Don't
take any notice of him, Mr
Windrush," she said. "He's just a bit
spoilt. He can't help being rude."

"Well," said the old man, "I hope you won't be disappointed. My work looks very rough and plain."

When Holly saw the skateboard lying on Mr Windrush's workbench, she wasn't just surprised; she was *astonished*. She jumped, just as if somebody had popped out from behind the sofa and shouted Hey!

Because the skateboard was *exactly* like the one she had been riding in her dreams, right down to the round buttons on the top! All she could say was, "Gosh, Mr Windrush! I don't *believe* it! Thank you, thank you, thank you!"

It made Mr Windrush very happy
to see how pleased Holly was. He
shut the gate after her, gave it a
contented little pat and went
indoors.

Richard was busy showing off, so he didn't notice that where the tips of Mr Windrush's fingers had tapped the gate, two little branches had sprung up and sprouted rainbow-coloured leaves and clusters of chocolate fudge bars.

Chapter Four

"What a piece of *junk*!" laughed Richard, when he saw Holly's new skateboard.

Holly took no notice. She lay on
her skateboard and enjoyed the
lovely curvy feeling she got as it
picked up speed down the slope.

"Too peasy!" shouted Richard.
"Watch me and I'll show you what
you can do on a *real* skateboard!"

He turned his hat round and
showed Holly how he did
Standies, Kneelies,
Wheelies and Jumpies.
He went really fast
and he never fell
off, not once.

Then he showed
her the big lump of
plastic at the back, so
you could stamp down
and make the board jump up.
"Bet you haven't got *this*," he said.

"I haven't got any plastic, but I
have got these special buttons," said
Holly. She got off her board and
pointed to the four round steel
buttons set into the wood.

Richard laughed and said they were just screwheads. "They hold the wheels to the board, Carrot Cake!" he scoffed. "*Anybody's* got those. They're not special. Look!"

He pressed down hard on one of his and showed her the white cross-shaped dent the screwhead made in his fingertip.

Holly had been thinking. Her birthday skateboard looked exactly the same as her dream skateboard – but perhaps it wouldn't *do* the same things in real life. Still, she held her breath, thought of her very favourite drink – and firmly pressed the top button on the left.

Chapter Five

Suddenly Holly was sipping
something delicious through a pink
bendy straw – a cold Coca-Cola
with a bubble gum ice-cream float
and a cherry on top.

"Would *you* like one of these?" she asked.

Richard was so surprised, he fell flat on his big bottom. "Gimme one!" he shouted.

"Please," said Holly.

Richard had to say the word, even though he hated it.

"Please," he begged.

Holly pressed the button again
and quick as a flash, Richard had
a paper cup full of the most
wonderful drink he had ever tasted –
cold and fizzy, with a
really big scoop of
the best bubble
gum ice-cream
ever. *Ever!*

Would you
like one of
these?

He couldn't
believe his
eyes. "Where
did this come
from?" he
demanded.

"I just pressed one of the special buttons, that's all," explained Holly. She sucked hard and made the Coke rattle in the bottom of her cup. "Ahhhh!" she gasped as she finished. "Just what I needed."

She put the empty paper cup
down on her skateboard, and as
soon as it touched the dull brown
wood, the cup went {}{}{}{}{}{}
and vanished.

Richard's mouth dropped open in
amazement.

"Let's go skateboarding!" laughed
Holly.

Chapter Six

For a minute, when Holly seemed
to be doing magic tricks, Richard
was lost for words. But as soon as
he heard her say, "Let's go
skateboarding!" he found his
voice again.

"Watch me!" he yelled, dropping his cup. "Because this is going to be *hard*, Miss Special Buttons!"

He raced down the slope, screaming his head off, jigged to avoid a pothole, bent his knees and neatly bounced the skateboard up over a kerb, before spinning it round and stopping it in a flurry of dust in front of the garages.

"Try *that* on your stupid piece of wood," he panted.

Holly lay face down, her legs sticking out like a frog's.

That made Richard laugh. She took no notice, but pointed herself down the slope, right at Richard, and kicked off with her toes.

With her nose just above the road, she was soon going even faster than Richard had done.

As
Holly
rushed
nearer, her
red hair flying out
behind her, Richard
started to get nervous.

If she didn't do something soon –
drag her baseball boots along the
ground or roll off sideways – she
would crash into the kerb, or
be smashed to pieces
against one of
the garage
doors!

Chapter Seven

Richard put his arm over his head and made himself as small as he could, expecting to be bowled over like a skittle.

That was when Holly pressed a
button and her skateboard lifted its
nose and took off like a plane.

It rose smoothly over the roofs of
the garages, and then soared higher
to skim the tops of some trees.

Holly looked down at the
cottages below, shrunk to the size
of toys. Richard looked no bigger
than an earwig. Holly pulled up the
nose of the skateboard and looped
the loop. Then she leaned,
swooping down to snatch a black
and white feather from an empty

magpie's nest, and stuck it in her
hair. Pink smoke came out of the
back of the skateboard and she
wrote her name in joined-up letters
in the sky. Then she dived and
landed expertly on the road before
rolling down to where Richard was
still glued to the spot.

"Let's go in and have some lunch
now, shall we?" Holly said, cool as a
Coca-Cola with a bubble gum ice-
cream float.

Chapter Eight

All through lunch Richard sat looking
at the magpie feather in Holly's hair
and wondering how he could get
the magic skateboard off her.

Finally, he had a very cunning idea.
When the car came for him,
Richard ran up to Holly's mum and
gave her a big kiss (which he had

never done before) and said, "Thank you very much for having me," (which he had never done before) and then he said, "Before I go, I would like to give Holly my fabulous, expensive skateboard and I'll just have her ugly old home-made one. How about that?"

Holly was too surprised to answer, and as for her mum and dad, they thanked Richard for coming, thinking what a lucky girl Holly was to have such a generous cousin.

Chapter Nine

Holly wandered out into the garden with Richard's skateboard and sighed a sad sigh.

"What's the matter, Holly?" came
a voice from the other side of the
fence. "Has your cousin left you?"

"I hope you won't be upset, Mr
Windrush," sniffed Holly, "but
Richard's taken the lovely
skateboard you made for me and
left me his."

"I'm not at all upset, Holly," said
Mr Windrush. "As a matter of fact,
I'd say you made a jolly good swap.
May I have a closer look?"

Holly passed it over the fence. Mr
Windrush held it just with the tips of
his fingers, touching the beautifully
smooth wood and feeling the cool
metal strip along its edge. "Why, this
is a *dream* of a skateboard," he
smiled, as he handed it back.

When she took it in her arms
once more, Holly was surprised to
notice that it had four round steel
buttons where the screwheads
had been!

"Happy skyboarding, Holly!" said
Mr Windrush.

Chapter Ten

Meanwhile, out on the motorway, there was a big traffic jam.

And in the middle of the big traffic jam there was a big car.

And in the back seat of the big
car there was a big rude boy with
a big bottom.

And the big boy with the big
bottom let out a big scream.

Because no matter how hard he pressed the buttons on his home-made skateboard, all he got was a little white cross-shaped dent on the tip of his finger!